Atiyya Shaw

TWELVE SILVER CUPS
AND
OTHER STORIES

Twelve Silver Cups

and
Other Stories

by

ENID BLYTON

Illustrations by

DOROTHY HAMILTON

AWARD PUBLICATIONS

For further information on Enid Blyton please contact www.blyton.com

ISBN 0-86163-142-0

First published 1947 as *Enid Blyton's Lucky Storybook*
by Brockhampton Press Limited

This edition entitled *Twelve Silver Cups and Other Stories*
published by permission of The Enid Blyton Company

First published 1985
15th impression 1999

Published by Award Publications Limited,
27 Longford Street, London NW1 3DZ

Printed in Hungary

CONTENTS

1

She Couldn't tell the Time!

Emily loved to go into the park to play with all her friends. She loved to go for walks, too, wheeling her doll's pram, either down the country lanes or into the little country town, where the buses stopped at the corner.

Emily was eight, and she couldn't tell the time! She simply wouldn't learn. She would stare at the clock when Mother asked her what the time was, and say all sorts of ridiculous things. When Mother said, 'I'm sure it's bedtime. What does the clock say?' Emily would say 'It says two o'clock.'

And when Mother said, 'Isn't it schooltime?' Emily would stare at the big round clock and say 'It's a quarter past seven, I think.'

Her Mother really began to be cross with her, because a big girl of eight should certainly tell the time. Also, as Emily *never* knew the time she was always late in from play or from her walks. Then Mother would have to keep her dinner hot for her, and that was a nuisance when she was busy.

'Emily, you *must* come in at the right time,' Mother would say. 'You *must* learn when it is half-past twelve and half-past four and half-past six. Then you will know that it is time to come home to dinner or tea, or for bed.'

Emily didn't want to learn the time. She didn't want to stop playing or walking, especially at bedtime. So she looked sulky and said that telling the time was just a nuisance!

'Very well,' said Mother, 'if you won't learn to tell the time, you can't go out to play or for a walk.'

'Oh please, Mummy!' said Emily. 'Please let me. The other children will tell me the time.'

'They always seem to tell you wrongly,' said Mother. 'Or else you ask them too late. No, Emily. You really *must* learn!'

Well, Emily begged and begged her Mother to let her go out to play in the park the next day, which was Saturday, and she looked so miserable about it that her Mother really didn't know what to do.

And then she suddenly had a very good idea. 'Now listen to me, Emily,' she said. 'You may go – but only if you take the old alarm clock with you. I shall wind up the alarm and set it for half-past twelve. I shall put it into your dolls' pram and then, as soon as the alarm bell rings you will know it is half-past twelve, and you will come straight home. Do you understand?'

Emily was rather astonished. She nodded her head. 'Yes Mummy,' she said. 'I'll take the clock. Then I really shall know when it's half-past twelve.'

So Mother took the clock from the mantlepiece and wound it up. She set the alarm to go off at half-past twelve, and put the clock into Emily's dolls' pram.

'Now there is no excuse for you not to be home in time for dinner,' she said.

Emily set off for the park. She didn't tell anyone about the alarm clock in her pram. In fact, she soon forgot about it. She played with her friends, and they fed the ducks and had a swing on the swings.

The morning flew by - and then, at exactly half-past twelve, there came such a noise from the dolls' pram! R-r-r-r-r-r-ing! R-r-r-r-r-ing! R-r-r-r-ring!

All the children stopped in surprise. 'What's that?' said Tom.

'Sounds like a bell of some sort,' said Lucy.

'It's coming from Emily's pram!' said Harry in amazement. He ran over to it. Sure enough the noise came from there. 'R-r-r-ing!'

'Whatever is it, Emily?' asked the children, crowding round.

'It's the alarm clock,' said Emily.

'*Alarm* clock!' said Harry. 'What do you want to bring out an alarm clock for?'

'Well, it's because I'm always late for meals,' said Emily. 'And I can't tell the time. So mother has put the alarm clock in my pram to tell me when it's half-past twelve.'

The children screamed with laughter. It seemed to them the funniest thing in the world for a little girl to have an alarm clock among her dolls. They laughed and laughed. Emily went rather red.

'It's nothing to laugh about,' she said crossly, and wheeled her pram home. For the first time in her life she was in time for dinner.

'Good !' said Mother. 'So the alarm clock told you the right time. Splendid! Go and wash your hands. You can go and play in the park again this afternoon, if you take the clock with you.'

Well, Emily somehow didn't want to take the clock with her, but Mother wouldn't let her go without it. She wound up the alarm again for Emily, and set it to ring at half-past four. Then she tucked it up into the pram again.

She couldn't tell the time!

When she met the other children they remembered the alarm clock that had made them jump that morning, and they ran to the pram.

'Here comes Alarm-Clock Emily!' they cried. 'What time is it going off, Emily?'

'Half-past four,' said Emily. And so it did. R-r-r-r-ing! R-r-r-r-ring! R-r-ring!

All the children shouted and jumped round the pram in glee. They really thought it was a huge joke. Emily went red again, and felt impatient with them. Harry looked at her.

'Do you mind us laughing at you?' he asked.

'Well, I don't like it very much,' said Emily. 'But my Mother says she won't let me come out to play unless I take the alarm clock with me to tell me the time.'

'I should have thought it would be much easier to learn to tell the time yourself,' said Harry. 'I think you're a baby not to be able to tell it – and you're eight! I could tell it when I was six.'

'I could if I wanted to,' said Emily, going red again. 'I wish I had learnt now.'

'Well, I'll teach you if you like,' said Harry.

And that evening, after tea, Harry took Emily to the big park clock and made her learn the time. It was very easy after all!

So, on Monday, when Emily wanted to go and play in the park after tea, and her Mother took down the alarm clock, Emily shook her head.

'You needn't give me that, Mother,' she said. 'I can tell the time.'

'Are you sure?' said her mother.

'Quite,' said Emily. 'Look, Mother, it's twenty past five. See how well I can tell the time!'

'Well, I'll try you this once,' said Mother, putting the clock back on the mantelpiece. 'Be home at half-past six, please.'

Well, Emily kept looking at the park clock, you can guess! It said ten to six, once when she looked, then six o'clock - and quarter-past six the next time, and almost half-past six the last time.

'I must go,' said Emily to the other children.

'But your alarm clock hasn't gone off yet,' said Lucy in surprise.

'I don't need it,' said Emily. 'I can tell the time as well as you can, Lucy.'

So she could - and so she can! She

doesn't need the alarm clock any more, and she is always punctual for meals and bedtime. Wasn't it a good idea to make her take an alarm clock in her pram!

2

He Lost His Tail!

Dobbin was the nursery horse. He was made of wood, and he stood on a stand that had four wheels. He had quite a nice mane, and a fine whisk of a tail.

He was a very naughty horse. He behaved quite all right so long as Jane and Ronald were playing in the nursery, but as soon as they were away, he went quite mad.

He rushed round the nursery, putting all the rugs crooked, and giving the little farmyard animals a terrible fright, for if he ran over one, it might break. He once jumped up into the air on his four wheels and sprang right over the dolls' house - but one of his wheels knocked the chimney and it fell off.

The other toys were angry with him. 'Look at that!' said the rabbit 'Do you

He Lost His Tail!

call that funny, knocking off a chimney like that?'

'Yes, I think it's *very* funny,' said the wooden horse, and he threw up his head and neighed so loudly with laughter that the toys rushed into the cupboard in a fright.

Dobbin used to chew things too, when the children were out of the nursery. He chewed the big doll's frock when she wasn't looking and made a great hole in it. He chewed the pink cat's tail in half, and once he even tried to chew the rabbit's tail when he was asleep in a corner - but the engine of the train saw him and went over and whistled loudly in the rabbit's ear, so he woke up in time to stop the wooden horse from eating *all* his tail!

Now one day Dobbin did something very naughty indeed. He said he was tired of being in the nursery, and he wanted to go into the garden for a walk.

'You can't do that!' cried the toys. 'You know you mustn't.'

But Dobbin only kicked up his heels and laughed. 'I'm off!' he said. And sure enough he galloped away on his wooden stand, out of the nursery door, down the long passage outside, out of the garden door, and into the garden! The toys crowded to the window to watch him.

He nibbled some flowers in the beds. He ate a lettuce. He trampled on the wallflowers that the gardener had neatly put out in the big round bed. He galloped all down the path and back, neighing like mad.

'It's a good thing that everyone is out today,' said the rabbit, 'I can't *think* what the children would say if they saw Dobbin behaving like that. Dobbin! Dobbin! Come back at once!'

But Dobbin didn't! He slipped through a hole in the fence and went into the field. But, dear me, the farmer was there, and Dobbin had to stand perfectly still, because the rule is that no toy must come alive when there are people to watch them. So there he stood in the field, looking like a perfectly good horse instead of a very naughty one.

Ah, but wait! Who is this coming scampering up to have a look at Dobbin? It is Gertie the goat! She was very curious to see what this creature was that had come into her field and suddenly stopped so still. She sniffed Dobbin all over from his nose to his tail.

And then she started to eat his tail! He couldn't do anything about it - he stood there trembling with fright and anger, and Gertie the goat ate the whole of his tail till there wasn't a single hair left.

Then she left him, and went to go home with the farmer. The gate was shut and Dobbin was alone once more. Crying big tears of rage he galloped through the hole in the fence, down the garden, and back to the nursery again.

And there he told the toys how he had lost his tail. He cried and cried about it. He begged them to make him a new one. He talked about it all day and all night till the toys were really tired of it.

'It serves you right, Dobbin, because you have often chewed *us*,' said the pink cat. 'Look at *my* tail – you ate half of that!'

'Yes – but I did leave you half,' wept Dobbin. 'And the goat hasn't left me even one hair of my tail. Oh, what shall I do, what shall I do? Please, please do get me another tail Toys. I shall cry all day and night till you do.'

'Oh, goodness gracious!' groaned the toys. 'If he cries all day and night, what a misery he will be! What *can* we get him for a tail?'

Well, they tried all kinds of things. They took the hairs from Jane's hair-brush and stuck them on to him but they soon came off. Then they pulled some hairs from a broom that someone had left in the passage – but they couldn't get enough, and Dobbin said he looked silly with a tail like that, so they threw the hairs into the waste-paper basket.

'You are an old fusser,' said the rabbit. '*I* can't think what tail to give you.'

And then the pink cat had a wonderful idea. At the top of the cupboard was an old feather-brush. Surely that would make a most wonderful tail!

'Look!' said the pink cat, pointing to the brush. 'That old feather-brush is never used – what about giving it to Dobbin?'

Dobbin liked the look of it, so the blue

monkey climbed up to the top shelf and brought down the old feather-brush. The toys stuck it into the hole where his tail had been, and the feathers looked just like a very thick tail.

'Oh, I'm proud of myself, I'm proud of myself,' cried Dobbin, galloping round the nursery in joy. 'Look at my wonderful tail! Aren't I a fine horse?'

Well, he really looked very funny with a bunch of feathers for a tail, but none of the toys liked to say so, because they were so tired of Dobbin being miserable without a tail. So they just giggled by themselves in corners whenever he galloped by, and he didn't see them laughing at all.

But, dear me, when Jane and Ronald came back to their nursery, how they stared to see Dobbin's tail! 'It's made of feathers!' they cried. 'Look – he's got a feather-tail! Oh, how comical! He's a bird-horse!'

And they laughed till the tears ran down their cheeks. Dobbin was very angry. 'I won't have a feather-tail now!' he neighed . 'Take it away.'

But they wouldn't; and as Dobbin couldn't possibly get his head round to his tail to bite it off, he still wears it. Every night he tries to get that tail off, and he nearly breaks his wooden neck in half, trying to make it reach to his tail. But he never can.

'It's no use, Dobbin,' say the toys. 'You wanted a new tail, and you wouldn't be happy till you got one so now you can keep it. It serves you right for being so naughty and galloping out of the nursery into the garden when you knew you weren't allowed to!'

If ever you see a wooden horse with a feather-brush tail, you'll know how he got it – but don't let him see you laughing at it, or he'll be *most* upset with you!

3

Blackberry Tart

Janey was very pleased because Ellen, who lived next door, had asked her and three other children to go on a blackberry picnic.

'Bring a big basket,' said Ellen. 'My mother knows a fine place for blackberries, and we are going to take tea with us. It will be great fun! We shall all bring our blackberries home, and our mothers will make us blackberry tart for our dinner next day.'

'Oooh!' said Janey, who loved blackberry tart. 'How lovely! I *shall* be excited this afternoon.'

But before the afternoon came, poor Janey had an accident. Mother had asked her to go and fetch some butter from the dairy down the road. So down she went to get it – and poor Janey fell off the kerb on to her knees and cut them very badly.

She didn't cry till she got home. Mother was very sorry indeed. She bathed her knees and bandaged them.

'Dear me, look at the butter!' Mother said. 'You fell on that too, Janey – it is a funny shape!'

That made Janey laugh – but she was soon in tears again, because Mother said she wouldn't be able to go to the blackberry picnic that afternoon.

'Darling, you can't possibly,' said Mother. 'You really couldn't walk all the way to the blackberry wood. Your knees are quite bad.'

Well, Janey begged and begged – but

it wasn't any use. Mother was right about the knees. Janey couldn't walk very well, and she would never get to the blackberry wood.

'I did so want to go to the picnic,' said Janey, crying bitterly. 'I did want to bring home lots of ripe blackberries for you, Mother. Now I shan't have a blackberry tart.'

'I'll buy some blackberries and make a tart for you,' said Mother.

'They don't taste the same,' sobbed Janey.

'Now don't be silly,' said Mother. 'You shall have a nice little picnic with Angela your doll this afternoon. You can squeeze through the hedge into the field at the bottom of the garden, and I will give you a picnic-basket all for yourself. You shall have tomato sandwiches, a piece of chocolate cake, and four sugar biscuits.'

'Oh, I shall like that!' said Janey, cheering up, and she went to dress Angela in picnic clothes, so that it wouldn't matter if she got dirty.

Janey felt sad again when she saw the other children going off for their picnic. But Mother quickly packed her picnic-basket for her, and Janey set off down the garden, limping a little because her knees hurt her. She put Angela through the hole in the hedge and then squeezed through after her with the basket.

Janey felt hungry, so she decided to have her picnic straight away. She went over to the other side of the field and sat on a grassy bank there. She

Blackberry Tart

undid her packet of sandwiches.

They tasted lovely. So did the chocolate cake. Janey saved the four sugar biscuits till last - and it was just as she was eating these that she suddenly saw the blackberries.

Janey stared as if she couldn't believe her eyes! On the hedge not far off grew blackberry brambles - and on these brambles were the largest, ripest blackberries that Janey had ever seen! They were thicker than she had ever seen too, growing in black clusters together.

Nobody came into that field except the farmer and his two horses, so nobody had seen the blackberries. There they were, waiting to be picked!

'Oh!' said Janey in delight. 'Look at them! I can pick enough to fill my basket! Won't Mother be surprised! Now we shall have our blackberry tart after all!'

She got up and limped over to the brambles. She began picking as fast as she could. Some of the berries went into her mouth - and they *were* delicious!

But most of them went into the basket.

When the basket was almost full and quite heavy, Janey squeezed back through the hedge and into her own garden again. She went up to the house and called Mother.

'I'm in the front garden!' cried Mother. So Janey went there - and just as she got there all the other children came running home with their baskets of blackberries.

'Hallo, Janey!' they cried. 'It *was* bad luck that you couldn't come blackberrying with us! Look what we've got!'

'And look what I've got!' said Janey proudly, and she showed them her basket full of the big ripe berries.

'Good gracious!' said Ellen. 'They are far better than ours! Wherever did you get them?'

'Mother let me have a picnic all to myself in the field at the back,' said Janey. 'And whilst I was having it I saw these blackberries. Aren't I lucky?'

'You *are!*' said all the others. 'Oh, Janey, we wish we'd been with you, instead of in the blackberry wood. Your berries are far bigger than ours.'

'Well, it was a good thing I fell down after all,' said Janey. 'It's funny how bad things turn into good things sometimes!'

'It depends how you behave about the bad things,' said Mother with a laugh. 'If you'd been silly and sulky about not going on the picnic with the others, and hadn't gone off by yourself to the field, you'd never have found the lovely big blackberries. Well, I'll make you a fine tart to-morrow.'

She did – a big juicy one, full of the ripe blackberries. Janey is going to eat it with cream. I wish I could have a slice too, don't you?

4

The Bonfire Folk

Peter and Jean were running home from school one day when they passed the cobbler's shop. Mr. Knock the cobbler was sitting cross-legged in his window, mending somebody's shoes.

His glass window was closed, for it was a cold day. Peter knocked on it, for he and Jean always liked to have a smile from the old cobbler. He had eyes as blue as forget-me-nots, and whiskers as white as snow.

Mr. Knock looked up and smiled, then beckoned the children inside. They opened the door and walked in, sniffing the good smell of leather.

'Did you want us, Mr. Knock?' asked Peter.

'Yes,' said Mr. Knock. 'I want to

know if you'll do an old man a good turn. My boy's ill and there are three pairs of shoes to be sent out. Do you think you and Jean could leave them for me on your way home?'

'Of course, Mr. Knock,' said Peter. 'We'd love to. Where are they?'

The old cobbler gave three parcels to them. 'That's for Captain Brown,' he said. 'That's for Mrs. Lee - and that little one is for Mrs. George's baby. You know where they all live, don't you?'

'Yes, Mr. Knock!' said the children, pleased. It was fun to play at being errand-boys! They rushed off with the parcels, and left them at the right houses. Then they went home to dinner. On their way to afternoon school they went to see Mr. Knock again.

'We left all your parcels safely for you,' said Peter.

'Thank you kindly,' said Mr. Knock. 'Now what would you like for a reward?'

'Nothing!' said Jean at once. 'We did it for you because we liked you. We don't want to be paid.'

'Well, I won't pay you,' said Mr. Knock, his blue eyes shining. 'But I happen to know something you badly want and maybe I'll be able to help you to get it. I know that you want to see the fairy folk, don't you?'

'Oooh, yes,' said both children at once, 'but we never have.'

'Well, I'll tell you a time *I* saw them,' said Mr. Knock, almost in a whisper. 'I saw them one cold December night, my dears – all toasting themselves beside my father's bonfire at the bottom of the garden. I've never told anyone till to-day - but now I'm telling you, for maybe you'll see them there too!'

Well! The children were so surprised that they could hardly say a word. They went off to school full of excitement. Daddy was at home that day and meant to make a bonfire, they knew. Suppose, just suppose they saw the little folk round the flames?

They went down to look at the bonfire after school. Daddy said he was going to let it out soon, and the children were disappointed. They ran off to some woods nearby, and, in the half-dark, managed to find some dry fir-cones. 'We'll use these to keep the fire in after tea,' said Jean. 'They burn beautifully.'

They placed a little pile of them beside the still-burning fire, and ran in to tea - but afterwards Auntie Mollie came and the two children had to stay and talk to her. It was their bedtime before they could think of going down to the bonfire again.

'Let's creep down now and see if anyone is there,' said Jean. 'I *would* so like to see. It's very cold and frosty to-night - maybe there will be one or two of the little folk there already.'

They put on their coats, their hats, and their scarves. They opened the garden door softly. They crept down the garden, walking on the grass so that their feet should make no noise.

'The bonfire is still burning,' whispered Jean. 'It didn't go out after all. Can you see anyone there?'

The children went round a hedge and came in sight of the fire. It was burning brightly, and the smoke swirled away from it, smelling delicious. Jean and Peter stopped and looked.

'There's Whiskers, our cat, sitting by

it!' said Jean in a delighted whisper. 'And look - there's the cat next door too! Both warming their toes!'

'What's that the other side?' whispered back Peter. 'I think - I really do think it's a brownie!'

It was! He was a tiny little man with a long beard and twinkling eyes. He was throwing fir-cones on the fire. No wonder it was burning brightly!

'It's the fir-cones we collected!' said Jean. 'How lovely! Oh, look - here's someone coming!'

Somebody came out of the shadowy bushes and sat down by the fire. It was an elf with long shining wings. She spoke to the cats and the brownie and they all nodded to her. They knew one another, it was quite certain. The fairy had brought some bundles of small twigs with her and these she threw every now and again on the fire, making it burn even more brightly.

Then a hedgehog came, and a rabbit. They sat down by the bonfire, and the rabbit held out both his paws to the flames. Jean and Peter thought he looked lovely.

'Isn't this exciting?' whispered Jean. 'I never thought we'd see all this! Do you suppose everybody's bonfires have bonfire folk around them at night?'

'I expect so,' said Peter. 'Oh, Jean - do let's go and speak to them all! I'm sure they won't be frightened.'

The two children left the hedge they were standing by and walked softly to the bonfire. Nobody saw them at first - and then the two cats pricked up their ears, spied them both, and shot away like shadows.

Peter caught hold of the brownie and held him tightly. 'Don't be afraid,' he said. 'I just want to speak to you. This is our bonfire and we are so pleased to see you come and warm yourselves by it. I am glad you used the fir-cones to make it burn brightly.'

'Oh, did *you* leave the fir-cones?' said the brownie. 'How kind of you! The fire was nearly out, but the dry cones just got it going again nicely. You're sure you don't mind us warming ourselves here? It's so very cold tonight – and these garden bonfires are so useful to us little folk.'

'You come whenever you like,' said Peter, letting go the brownie, now that the little man knew the children were friends. For a few minutes they all sat there together, and the rabbit was just about to jump on to Jean's knee when the children heard their mother calling.

'Peter! Jean! You naughty children! Surely you haven't gone out into the cold garden! Come to bed at once.'

'Good-bye!' said the children to the bonfire folk. 'Tell everybody to use our fire each night. We like to know you are there.' And off they ran to bed.

They love to think of all the little bonfire-folk sitting round the smoky fire in the garden. Do *you* ever have a bonfire? Well, maybe the little folk are round yours too, warming their toes on a winter's evening! Wouldn't I love to see them!

5

The Old Toad and the Spider

There was once a sly old toad who lived in a damp ditch at the bottom of a large garden. Each spring he crawled to the nearby pond and played with the other toads there. When he was tired of that, he went back to his ditch to wait for flies and caterpillars to come along for his dinner.

One summer his ditch dried up, and the toad felt hot and uncomfortable. So he left the ditch and crawled through the hedge.

Soon he came to an orchard, where the leaves of the trees threw a thick green shade. The grass below was long and wet. The toad liked it. It felt cool to his brown back and he liked the wetness. He sat beneath an apple tree and waited for flies.

'There are plenty in this orchard,' said the toad to himself. 'I shall grow fat and comfortable.'

Now just above him lived a spider. She was old and big and cunning. She had spun more webs than she could remember, and had caught thousands of flies. She was not pleased when she saw the toad.

'The tiresome old creature!' she said to herself. 'This is the best place in the whole orchard for flies. That is why I have made my web here. It is *my* place, not his.'

So she spoke to the old toad from her

place in the middle of the web.

'Toad! You must find another hunting-ground. I have spun my web here every summer for years!'

The toad blinked up at her with his beautiful coppery eyes. 'I shall stay here,' he said. 'There are flies enough for both.'

The spider watched him. A large bluebottle came by and the toad sat as still as a stone. The bluebottle settled on a grass at the edge of the spider's web - but before the spider could dart on it the toad shot out his long sticky tongue, hit the fly with the end of it, and drew it quickly into his mouth! He swallowed, blinked - and the fly was gone!

'*Very* nice!' said the toad. '*Much* better than going to the trouble of making a web! My tongue is fastened to the front of my mouth instead of to the back, so I can fling it out quite a long way. That was a most tasty bluebottle, spider.'

The spider was very angry. She saw the toad catch fly after fly with his quick tongue, and only a few of the smaller ones came into her web.

Then came two or three wet days, and no flies were about. The toad grew very hungry. The spider saw that he was thinner and she spoke to him.

'Toad, do you like the water? From where I swing in my web I can see the pond, and there are all kinds of flies hovering over the surface. Why do you not go and catch a few till the weather becomes warm again?'

The toad knew that many flies hovered over the pond in the summer. He thought about it. Then slowly he crawled away to the pond. The spider was delighted. She knew something that the toad did not know. She knew that the white ducks came to the pond every day for a swim.

'They will eat the toad!' she said. 'That will be the end of him. Then I shall be able to catch all the orchard flies myself.'

The toad came to the pond. He went in with a flop. He swam about gracefully, enjoying the water. The spider had spoken truthfully, for there were a great many flies skimming the top of the water. The toad ate as many as he wanted.

'It was friendly of the spider to tell me,' he thought. But he quite changed his mind when midday came. For then the eight white ducks came too, quacking and waddling, longing for their

swim! They flopped into the water and paddled their legs so that they swam all about. Some of them put their heads down to see what they could find below the surface. The toad was most alarmed.

He swam quickly to a rock he knew, and squeezed himself under it. But a duck had seen him and came probing under the rock with her beak. The toad only just got out at the other side in time. He swam to the side of the pond and crawled into a mass of rushes. But when the ducks came waddling round that side he had to jump into the water again and swim all the way across the pond in a great hurry.

He crawled out, very tired. He was angry with the spider, very angry indeed. He knew she had played a trick on him. He made his way back to the orchard, meaning to break her web and eat her.

But the spider was watching for him. She curled herself up, with her eight legs beneath her, and lay as if she were dead, under a piece of loose bark near her web. The toad lumbered up, his copper eyes gleaming.

He put up a paw and broke the lovely web. Then he looked for the spider. When he found her, lying on her back looking as dead as could be, he gave a croak.

'Dead! Ha, and a good thing too! Serve her right for playing me such a

trick! Well, I don't eat dead spiders, so I'll leave her there for the field-mice to eat.'

He went to find himself a good stone to crawl beneath, because the nights were growing a little chilly and he knew that soon the time would come when he must sleep for the winter. He must have a good stone then, or he might be found and eaten by some hungry animal.

As soon as he had gone, the spider came alive again, in the quick way that spiders have. Her legs straightened out, and she stood the right way up, her big eyes looking all around her. She saw the toad crawling under a stone.

She ran over to it. Above were twigs, and quickly the spider wove a big web just above the stone.

So, when the toad crawled out into the sun to catch a few autumn flies, he found the spider in the middle of a big web just above him.

'But you were dead!' he croaked, in surprise and dismay.

'Not really!' said the spider, and she

swung to and fro in her web. 'Not really!'

And now the cold days are coming

when the toad and the spider will sleep. You will find the spider crouching as if she were dead behind a loose piece of bark – and the toad will be asleep under his stone! Don't disturb them, for they are good friends of ours. In the spring they will wake again and try their tricks on one another. Who do you suppose will win?

6

Sally Simple's Matches

Sally Simple was very angry because she was always losing her matches. She wanted to light her candle, and the matches had gone again.

'Where are they, where are they?' cried Sally Simple, stamping all over the place. 'I put them down by the candle, I know I did - and now they're gone again! Nobody has been here - I'm the only one in the house, so where, where, where have those matches gone?'

She found them at last on the window-ledge, and then she remembered that she had lent them to old Mr. Twiddle to light his pipe when he went by that morning. He had given them back to her and she had popped them on the windowsill instead of putting them by her candle.

'Now this won't do,' said Sally sternly to herself. 'Sally, you waste half your time looking for your matches. In the morning you cannot find them to light the fire. At night you cannot find them for your candle. You can never find them unless you hunt for ages all over the place. Now be sensible, Sally

Simple, and think of a safe place to keep them in *always*.'

When Sally Simple talked to herself like that, she always listened. She thought for a moment and then she nodded.

'I know where I'll keep the matches,' she said. 'I'll put them in my apron pocket, and then they will always be with me. All I need to do is to slip my hand into my pocket and there the matches are!'

So she put the box there, and felt very pleased with herself. She felt so pleased that she hummed all day long as she worked. Then Dame Fanny came in to see her, and told her all the news. She stayed for a cup of tea, and after she went, Sally cleared away and washed up.

It began to get dark. Sally thought she would light the lamp. She went to the lamp table and felt about for the matches, which she sometimes put there. She had quite forgotten where she had put them.

They were not there. Sally was cross. 'Maybe I left them by the stove,' she said. But they were not there. Then she went to the candlesticks, but there were no matches there either.

'Bother, bother, bother!' said Sally. 'Now I must really go and borrow some, for I cannot see to hunt all over the place for the matches.'

So she went to Mother Grumps, her next-door neighbour. She knocked at the door. 'Please, could you lend me some matches?' she asked.

'I haven't any,' said Mother Grumps. 'Just used the last one to light my candle with. Sorry.'

So then Sally went to the house on the other side of her cottage and knocked on the door. Mr. Tweaky lived there. He opened the door, and was pleased to see Sally.

'Come in, come in,' he said. Sally stepped inside. 'And what can I do for you?' asked Mr. Tweaky.

'Well, I've come to borrow a box of matches, please,' said Sally. 'I can't find mine, and I must light my lamp.'

'There's my box over there,' said Mr. Tweaky. 'Just by you - look, Sally.'

Sally picked up the box - but alas it was empty! 'Oh dear - you must have

used the last one, Mr. Tweaky,' said Sally. 'Haven't you any more?'

'Yes, I've some in my store-cupboard upstairs,' said Mr. Tweaky. 'Bring the candlestick, Sally, and we'll look.'

Sally took the lighted candlestick and went upstairs with Mr. Tweaky. He opened the door of his big store-cupboard, but just as he did so the wind from the open window blew out the candle. They were in darkness.

'Oh dear!' said Sally. 'The candle's gone out.'

'Never mind,' said Mr. Tweaky. 'I think I know where the matches are. I'll get a chair because I think they are on the top shelf.'

So he got a chair and stood on it. He felt along the top shelf, and tried to find the packet of matches. But he couldn't find them. So he stood on tiptoe and tried to reach to the very back of the shelf - and over went the chair and down went poor Mr. Tweaky with a dreadful bump!

'Oh! Oh! I've hurt myself!' he cried. 'Bring a light, bring a light! I've hurt myself! Light the candle, and let me see what I've done!'

Sally Simple was dreadfully upset. She set the candlestick on the floor, and felt in her apron pocket for the matches. She struck one and lighted the candle. Then she looked at Mr. Tweaky.

He had bruised his leg and his arm

Sally Simple's Matches

very badly. Sally helped him down-stairs and put him on the couch. She bathed the bruises and put bandages on - and all the time Mr. Tweaky glared at her and seemed very angry indeed.

Sally couldn't understand it. 'Please Mr. Tweaky, why are you so cross?' she asked. 'It was not my fault that you fell off the chair, and I have been as kind as possible to you since you did.'

'I think you are a very bad person,' said Mr. Tweaky. Sally began to cry.

'Why?' she asked. 'I haven't done anything wrong.'

'Sally Simple, you came here to ask for a box of matches - you made me go upstairs to the store-cupboard, you made me stand on a chair in the dark and feel for my matches - and when I fell down and hurt myself, what did you do?'

'I lighted your candle to see what had happened to you,' sobbed Sally.

'Yes,' said Mr. Tweaky: 'you *took a box of matches out of your pocket,* Sally, and struck a match - after you had come to borrow *my* matches, and made me have this horrid accident. How dare you come to borrow matches when you've got some in your pocket!'

'Oh dear, oh dear, how foolish I am!' sobbed Sally. 'I'd forgotten where I'd put them till that very minute, really I had, Mr. Tweaky.'

'Please go home,' said Mr. Tweaky. 'I don't want puddles of tears all over my carpet. I'm very upset with you, Sally Simple.'

So Sally went home. And will you believe it, when she put her hand into her apron pocket to get the matches to light her own lamp, they weren't there! She had left them at Mr. Tweaky's. Well, well, well! So Sally had to go to bed in the dark that night, because she really didn't dare to go and ask Mr. Tweaky for them.

Now she ties them to her candlestick every day and they can't disappear. Poor Sally!

7

Twelve Silver Cups

Jeffery was a splendid runner, and at his school sports he always won all the running prizes. His father and mother felt very proud when he went up to get the silver cups that were the reward for the best runner.

'Really, Jeffery,' said his Mother, 'I shall have to have a special little cupboard made for you to keep your silver cups in! When you have twelve I will get you one.'

Jeffery already had eleven. So that year when he again won the prize for running he had his twelfth silver cup. How pleased he was!

'Now you'll have to get me that special cupboard you promised,' he said to his mother.

'I certainly will,' she said. And in a week's time a nice oak cupboard came, with a glass door in front. There were two big shelves inside, and Jeffery proudly arranged his cups on the top one.

'Plenty of room for more cups!' said his mother, smiling at him. 'Don't they look lovely, Jeffery?'

Jeffery was proud of his cupboard. His mother showed it to people when they came to tea, and Jeffery liked to see people looking at it and hear them say how nice the cups were.

And then, what do you think happened one night to those twelve silver cups? A burglar got into the house and stole them all! He hadn't time to take anything else because Spot the dog began to bark. Daddy woke up and heard a noise and tore downstairs – just in time to see a dark figure running down the garden.

Daddy switched on the light, and saw that Jeffery's cups were gone. He ran into the garden – but the man had disappeared. So Daddy rang up the police.

But nobody seemed to be able to get back those cups. Jeffery was very unhappy, because they were his and he had been proud of them. It had taken him years to win them, and now he would have to begin all over again to fill his oak cupboard.

The policeman took a lot of notes and asked a great many questions. But he didn't catch the thief, though he said he felt sure he knew who it was.

'But I've gone into his house and looked all around whilst I've been questioning him, and I can't see the cups anywhere,' said the policeman. 'Maybe he's hidden them somewhere and will go and get them when the fuss has died down!'

Two weeks went by and nothing was heard of the twelve silver cups. Then another bit of bad luck came to Jeffery. He lost his tortoise!

He had had Slowcoach, his tortoise, for six years, and was fond of the quaint old creature. Slowcoach would let Jeffery tickle him under the chin, and would always poke his head out when Jeffery whistled a special whistle. Now he was gone!

'Oh, Mother, wherever do you think he can be?' said Jeffery. 'I've hunted over every bit of the garden.'

'He must have escaped into someone else's garden,' said Mother. 'You know how tortoises wander, Jeff.'

'But the wire between our garden and the next garden's is quite all right,' said Jeffery. 'I've looked at it.'

'What about the wire at the end of the garden?' said Mother. 'That's not so strong as the side wire.'

Jeffery went to look at it, and he

looked very carefully indeed. Mother was right! The wire was not so strong there, and Spot had scraped at it and bent it back in one place so that he might get into the big ploughed field at the back.

'I guess that's where old Slowcoach got out!' said Jeffery to himself. 'Bother! He may be anywhere in that enormous field. Well - he's my pet and I'd better look for him.'

It was a cold day, and there was frost in the wind. Jeffery buttoned up his coat, climbed over the fence and went into the big field. He simply didn't know where to begin to look for his tortoise.

'His brown shell is so like the earth that I don't believe I'd see him if he was right under my nose!' said the boy. 'Hie, Spot! Come and help me! Find Slowcoach! Maybe your nose will find what my eyes can't!'

Spot squeezed through the hole in the wire and danced over the field, yelping. He sniffed here and there and then he and Jeffery both saw the same thing! In the middle of the field a piece of earth flew up into the air - and then another!

Jeffery ran over the furrows - and when he got to the place he laughed.

'It's old Slowcoach burying himself for the winter!' he said. 'What a long way you've walked over the field, Slowcoach!'

'Wuff!' said Spot, and danced round

the tortoise. There was nothing much to be seen of him except one hind leg, for he was now half buried.

Jeffery pulled Slowcoach gently out of the soil.

'Slowcoach, you have your own box of moss and bracken at home in the shed,' he said. 'That's where you sleep for the winter - not in a damp, cold field where you might be hoed up! Come along!'

Spot went to the hole and sniffed there. Then he began to scrape excitedly at the earth, and in a few moments Jeffery was spattered from head to foot with flying soil.

'Stop, Spot, stop!' he yelled. 'Are you thinking of burying yourself for the winter too? You're not a tortoise! Don't be silly!'

But Spot wouldn't stop. He went on and on digging - and then a strange thing happened. He pulled hard at a dirty brown rope, and yelped loudly.

Jeffery put the tortoise down and helped Spot. He pulled at the rope - and a sack came slowly up from the earth. Something inside it clinked.

Jeffery undid the rope and looked inside the little sack. And in it were his twelve silver cups! Yes - the thief had hurriedly buried them in the middle of the field, meaning to return for them when it was safe. There they all were in the dirty sack, very dull and tarnished, and with scratches here and there - but safe!

With Slowcoach in one hand, the sack over his shoulder, and Spot yelping round his feet excitedly, Jeffery rushed home.

'Mother! Mother!' he yelled, 'I've found my twelve silver cups! At least, Slowcoach really found them, and Spot

dug them up – but I've got them, I've got them, I've got them!'

He *was* so pleased, and so was his Mother. Now she has cleaned them beautifully, and Jeffery has stood them all neatly on the top shelf of his cupboard.

'Slowcoach shall have a nice new box to go to sleep in this winter,' said Jeffery. 'And Spot shall have a new

collar! I *am* pleased to have my cups back, Mother! I do wonder if the thief will know.'

The thief didn't know. He went digging in the field for the cups two nights later - and the policeman caught him. He won't go stealing twelve silver cups again!

8

The Cracker Fairies

Elsie and William were so unhappy that they cried streams of tears down their cheeks - and indeed, it wasn't surprising, because they both had bad colds on Christmas Day, and both had to stay in bed!

'It *is* bad luck!' said Mummy. 'But it's just no good letting you get up - you might be really ill. So you must try and be happy.'

But poor Elsie and Will found it very difficult to be happy. Their new toys were on their beds, but they didn't feel like playing with them. They could wind up their new train and new motor-cars and bus, but they couldn't let them run on the bed - they got caught in the sheets! So it really wasn't any fun at all.

Mummy was so busy, too, because Grannie and Grandpa, Auntie Ellen and Uncle Jim and their three children were all coming to tea that afternoon. She had such a lot of things to get ready that she really hadn't had much time for Elsie and William.

'Could John, Joan, and Jessie come to see us this afternoon when they come?' asked Elsie.

Mummy shook her head. 'No,' she said. 'You might give them your cold

and that would never do. I'm so sorry darlings: but we will give you a treat when you are better – and you must just be as cheerful as you can without any visitors to see you today.'

Now it so happened that twelve little fairies came by that way, and peeped in at the children's window. When they saw Elsie and William crying, they were most surprised.

'Look at that!' said the biggest fairy. 'Crying on Christmas Day! Whatever's

happened? Do you suppose they didn't get any presents?'

'They've plenty on their beds,' said the second fairy. 'They must be ill, poor children. What a shame! Let's go and play with them to cheer them up.'

So in at the window they went - but just as they were inside, behind the curtain, the bedroom door opened and the children's mother walked in. The fairies got a terrible fright. Wherever were they to hide?

On the chair nearby was a box of crackers. 'Quick!' whispered the biggest fairy. 'There are twelve crackers, look! We'll each slip inside one, and we won't be seen!'

So into the crackers they crept, right into the very middle, where caps and toys were waiting. They hid there, as quiet as mice, and didn't move at all in case the children's mother should see them.

'I wish we could have our crackers now,' said Elsie, with a sigh. 'I'm tired of lying here, without any excitement at all.'

'Well, you can have them if you like,' said her mother, and she put the box on the children's bed. 'Now I must go down and see how things are getting on. Be good!'

She went out of the door. Elsie took up a cracker and held it out to Will. 'Pull, Will!' she said. 'We'll see what is inside!'

They pulled hard - BANG! The cracker came in half with a loud pop - and out fell a fairy, a cap, and a toy. The children stared in the greatest astonishment and delight at the little fairy with her blue dress and blue wings.

She flew on to Elsie's hand. 'I've

come to play with you to cheer you up on Christmas Day,' she said. 'Pull the other crackers, and see what is in them.'

So Will and Elsie pulled a second cracker – BANG! Out fell another fairy, all in pink this time. She flew on to Will's hand and stood there, laughing up at him. He was simply delighted.

Well, one after another all those crackers were pulled, and out fell the twelve fairies, laughing and chattering, flying about the bed, and making such a cheerful bird-like noise!

'We'll wind up your toys and set them going on the floor for you to see, if you like,' said the biggest fairy. So down they all flew, and soon the engine, the motor cars and the bus were running busily over the floor. Then the second fairy, who was very good at reading, read a whole story to the children from one of the new books.

By that time it was dinner-time and the children's mother came in with their dinner. The fairies hid under the

pillows at once. Mummy was *most* surprised to see the children looking so happy and cheerful!

When they ate their dinner the twelve fairies sat round the edges of the two plates and nibbled crumbs of bread. It was so funny to see them. When Mummy came in again, they slipped under the sheet. Elsie nearly laughed out loud because one fairy tickled her leg!

'Now you must have your rest,' said Mummy, and she tucked them up. As soon as she had gone, the fairies slipped out from the bed. 'Where can we have a rest too?' they asked.

'Could you all get into my dolls' cot, do you think?' asked Elsie. They flew over to it. They scrambled in, put their tiny heads on the pillow, and were soon just as fast asleep as the two children.

They had tea with the children when they woke up, and when Mummy brought Elsie and William two balloons the fairies played with them all over the room. They flew in the air and

bumped the balloons up to the ceiling.

'You are so funny,' laughed Elsie. 'I've never seen anyone play with balloons like that before!'

Then it was time for the fairies to go. They kissed the children, and do you know what two of the fairies gave them – a tiny silver wand each, that would do magic!

Mummy found the wands under the pillow. 'I suppose these little things came out of the crackers?' she said. 'What dear little toys!'

'They *did* come out of the crackers!' Elsie whispered to Will. 'They came with the Cracker-fairies!'

9

Salt on a Bird's Tail

Have you ever heard that you can catch a bird if you put salt on its tail? I expect you have - and maybe you have tried to do it too.

There was once a little girl called Alice who loved birds very much. She fed them all through the winter, and she gave them water to drink and a bowl to bath in during the summer.

They grew very tame indeed, and the robin would perch on the handle of her garden spade whenever she left it sticking into the earth. But not one of the birds would let Alice hold it in her hand so that she might feel the warm body and fluffy feathers.

'I do so wish the birds loved me enough to trust me to pick them up gently,' Alice said to her Uncle Jim, who was also very fond of birds. 'I've never held a bird in my hand, Uncle - and they do look as if they would be so lovely to hold for a moment or two. I'd like to feel them against my neck, all soft and warm.'

'Well,' said Uncle Jim with a laugh, 'don't you know how to catch a bird, Alice? Just put salt on its tail, and you've got it!'

'Oh, really, Uncle Jim?' said Alice, in delight. 'I'll try then.'

So the very next day Alice went to the sideboard and took the little glass salt-cellar out. She emptied some of the salt into a paper sweet-bag and then put the salt-cellar back. Out she went into the garden.

'Now, where are there any birds?' thought the little girl. 'Oh – there's a sparrow on the lawn!'

She crept up to it, nearer and nearer – but the bird saw her and flew off with a chirrup of fright. Alice waited till another bird appeared.

'There's the pretty chaffinch on the grass,' she said. 'I'd love to catch him and hold him gently.' So she crept softly over the grass to where the chaffinch was pecking around.

She put her finger and thumb into

the bag of salt - but the chaffinch heard the little rustle of the paper and flew off with a whirr of his pretty wings.

Alice was very disappointed. She wondered if perhaps she ought to hide in the bushes - then the birds wouldn't see her. So she squeezed herself into a bush and waited patiently. A blackbird came and perched just above her head. He flicked his tail up and down. Alice quietly got ready a pinch of salt - but he suddenly saw her, gave his loud alarm-cry, and flew off.

'Bother!' said Alice. 'It's too bad. The birds see me and get a fright. Really it's silly of them, because they know I'm their friend!'

Then she thought it would be a good idea if she fetched some breadcrumbs and threw them down. The birds would come to get them and she could perhaps quickly throw a pinch of salt on their tails as they pecked about.

So she fetched some stale pieces of bread and broke them up into crumbs.

Soon the lawn was white with crumbs and the birds called to one another to come and feed.

Down flew three sparrows. Down flew the robin. The blackbird came after a good look round. Two thrushes came and hopped among the crumbs. Even the wagtail came, wagging his tail up and down in his merry way.

Alice was sitting on the grass, her bag of salt beside her. The birds came nearer and nearer. Alice had a pinch of salt ready. She suddenly threw it among the birds, hoping that some might fall on the tail of one of them. Then it would not be able to fly away and she could pick it up and love it.

But all the birds were scared when Alice raised her hand and threw something. They thought she was throwing a stone, and they flew off with chirrups and squawks. They could not understand why Alice was doing such queer things.

'She always seemed so friendly,' sang the blackbird to the thrush.

'She gives us water to drink and a bowl to splash in,' chirruped the sparrows. 'Why is she throwing things at us today?'

Alice was very upset that all the birds had flown. She went under the lilac bush and had a good cry.

'It's too bad,' she sobbed. 'I do so want to catch a bird by putting salt on its tail, but none of them will let me!'

Now a small elf lived in the bush, and he was most astonished to hear what Alice said. He was fond of the little girl, though she had never seen him -but he had often watched Alice giving food to the birds and pouring fresh water into their bathing-bowl.

'Dear me,' he said to himself. 'What a funny thing to cry about! Whoever heard of catching birds by putting salt on their tails? Well, now, I wonder if I can do anything about it?'

Now the elf had a friend. It was the little brown hedge-sparrow who had her nest in the hawthorn bush at the end of the garden. When Alice had

crept out from the lilac bush to try again with her salt, the elf flew quickly to the hedge-sparrow who was sitting on her nest.

'Hedge-sparrow,' said the elf, 'will you do something for me?'

'Of course!' said the little brown bird.

'Well, listen, said the elf. 'There is a little girl in the garden and she wants to catch a bird by putting salt on its tail, and she is very unhappy because she can't. Now do go and hop about in front of her, and let her put salt on your little brown tail. Then let her pick you up and hold you gently against her face so that she can feel how soft and warm you are.'

'But I should be afraid,' said the hedge-sparrow in alarm.

'You needn't be,' said the elf. 'She is the kindest girl in this village. Do do it, please.'

'What about my eggs?' asked the hedge-sparrow.

'I'll sit on them for a while and keep them warm,' said the elf. So the hedge-sparrow flew off and the elf cuddled himself down over the bright blue eggs. Off went the hedge-sparrow, still feeling very nervous. She saw Alice sitting patiently on the grass, with her little bag of salt in front of her.

The hedge-sparrow flew down and pecked up a crumb. She went nearer and nearer to Alice. Alice took a pinch of salt. Her eyes gleamed with delight. She felt sure she could put some on this little bird's tail!

She threw the salt. It fell on the hedge-sparrow's tail like snow. The little bird stayed quite still as if she were caught and could not move. Alice picked her up in her hand.

'Oh!' she cried in delight. 'I've caught a bird at last! Oh, you dear, soft little thing – you are as warm as new-made bread! Oh, how soft you are against my cheek!'

At first the hedge-sparrow was afraid, but when she felt how gentle and loving Alice was, she no longer felt nervous. She stayed quite still in the little girl's hand, her tiny heart beating like the quick ticking of a small clock.

'I don't want to hurt or frighten you,' said Alice. 'I only wanted to feel you. Now you shall fly away again. Have you a nest, little bird? How I would love to see it!'

The hedge-sparrow flew from Alice's hand and sang her a short sweet burst of song. She flew down the garden and perched on the hawthorn bush to make sure that Alice was following. She

wanted to show the little girl her beautiful eggs.

But do you know, when Alice looked for the nest, she saw, first of all, the elf! The hedge-sparrow had quite forgotten that the elf had promised to look after her eggs. Alice rubbed her eyes in amazement - and when she took her knuckles from her eyes, the elf was gone. But then Alice saw the four lovely blue eggs shining in the neat brown nest.

'Oh!' she said. 'They are as blue as the sky! Thank you, hedge-sparrow for showing me them. I've never seen such a lovely sight before!'

Alice rushed in to tell her mother - and Uncle Jim was there too.

'Oh, Mother! Oh, Uncle Jim!' cried Alice. 'I caught a bird by putting salt on its tail - and I held it in my hand - and it showed me its nest with four blue eggs in and there was an elf keeping the eggs warm for the bird too!'

How Uncle Jim laughed! 'My dear

child,' he said. 'It's just a joke that you can catch birds by putting salt on their tails. You can't really!'

'But I did, I tell you!' cried Alice. 'I did, I did!'

Yes – she certainly did, didn't she? I wonder if you'd be as lucky! You never know!

10

The Magic Motor Car

Cherry Village was a very happy little place till Mister Bong came to live there. It was beautiful in the spring-time when all the cherry trees were out, and it was fun to be there in the summer when the cherries were ripe. Then everyone had cherry-tart and cream.

But when Mister Bong came, he made himself a great nuisance. He talked so much. He borrowed such a lot of things from the village folk. He said such horrid things about them. In fact, he was very tiresome indeed.

'Here comes Mister Bong!' Gobo would say to Littlefeet. 'Quick! Let's run away before he sees us! He is sure to want to borrow something!'

And off they would go - but Mister Bong would be sure to see them and hurry after them to grumble about something or other.

He loved to see anything new that the folk of Cherry Village bought. When Gobo brought home a new wireless set, Bong knocked at his door, walked in, and spent the whole evening twiddling the knobs of the set - though poor Gobo was longing to try it himself.

When Tiptoe bought a new bicycle, Mister Bong borrowed it, and rode it to Heyho Town to see his aunt - and when he brought it back the bell was broken.

'You ought to pay for a new bell,' said Tiptoe crossly. But Mister Bong just laughed, went home and banged his door. And Tiptoe had to pay for a new bell herself.

But when Mister Bong borrowed Dame Jelly's garden-roller without asking, and lost it in the village pond, everybody said something must be done about him.

'But how did he lose the roller in the pond?' asked Gobo in surprise. He had been away for the day and hadn't heard what had happened.

'Well, you see, he went to borrow the roller one night, when Dame Jelly was asleep,' said Tiptoe. 'And, as you know, her house is at the top of the hill. Well,

just as he was setting off down the hill, Bong sneezed, and it was such a big sneeze that he let go the roller. It rolled by itself at a great speed down the hill, and went splash right into the pond.'

'And as the pond is big and deep, we can't see it anywhere, so it's quite lost,' said Littlefeet.

'Then it's certainly time that we did something about Bong,' said Gobo, frowning.

A small pixie called Dumbell began to giggle. The others stared at him. 'What's the matter?' asked Gobo.

'I've thought of something,' said Dumbell. 'My aunt has a motor car, and when I'm good she lets me use it. Now what about me bringing it here, giving everyone but Bong a nice ride – and then leaving it somewhere for him to borrow.'

'What's the use of that?' said Gobo.

'We'll leave a runaway spell in the seat,' giggled Dumbell, 'and as soon as Bong gets in, the car will run away with him for miles and miles and miles! After a hundred miles it will tip him out, and come back here to us.'

The little folk stared at Dumbell in

delight. It sounded a very good idea. Dumbell was at once sent off to borrow his aunt's car.

He soon came back in it, grinning all over his mischievous little face. He

sounded the horn loudly and everyone came running out.

'I'll give you all rides in turn,' shouted Dumbell. So first Gobo got in and had a ride, and then Littlefeet, and then Tiptoe. Mister Bong pushed his way through the crowd after that, and shouted out that *he* wanted a turn.

'Oh, no, I'm not giving *you* any rides!' said Dumbell cheekily. 'I don't want my car lost in the village pond, Mister Bong. That's what you do with things that are lent to you, don't you?'

So Bong was not allowed a ride at all, and he was very angry indeed, for he felt sure he could drive the little blue motor car just as well as Dumbell could.

'There!' said Dumbell, when everyone but Bong had had a nice drive round the village. 'That's all for today. I'll just put the car safely by this wall and go and have my supper.'

He put it beside a wall near Bong's house. Before he got out he pressed a runaway spell on to the driving-seat. It looked like a bit of yellow stamp-paper. Dumbell giggled, jumped out, and ran home to supper.

As soon as everyone was gone, Mister Bong ran out of his house. He went to the car, pleased to see it left so near his house. He got in and took hold of the wheel.

'I'll show Dumbell that I will have my turn in the car just like everyone else!' he said. He started off, and as soon as the little folk heard the sound of the car, they all rushed out of their houses to see what would happen.

'Good-bye, Bong! Good-bye, Bong!' they shouted, waving their hands in glee. Bong looked surprised. He meant to go once round the village, but somehow the car wouldn't go the way he wanted it to.

The car ran to the main road. Bong tried to turn it back to the village, but no, it wouldn't turn. 'R-r-r-r-r-,' it went, as if it were laughing at him.

'Good-bye, and good riddance!' yelled the folk of Cherry Village. Bong began to feel frightened. He didn't seem to be driving the car at all – it seemd to be driving him! Off he went down the main road, up a hill, and down the other side, going faster and faster and faster.

The little folk could no longer see him. They took hands and danced in a ring for joy. 'He's gone, he's gone!' they sang. 'Now we shall all be happy again!'

That night, going rather slowly, as if it were a little tired, the magic motor car came back again to Cherry Village. Everybody welcomed it. They patted its bonnet, they tied a ribbon to its

steering-wheel, and really made a great fuss of it.

'Thank you!' they said. 'Thank you! We shan't see Mister Bong again!'

And they won't. He was tipped out on a rubbish-heap in Goblin town over a hundred miles away – and now he is a servant to a family of goblins. Well, it serves him right – he shouldn't have been such a nuisance!

11

It Was Only a Little Thing

Daddy was sometimes not very pleased with John. John was careless, and didn't try to remember all he should.

'But, Daddy, they are only little things that I forget,' said John one day, when his Daddy had scolded him for forgetting to shut the garden gate and for leaving his new spade out in the rain.

'You never know when a little thing will turn into a big thing before you can stop it,' said Daddy. 'It's very often the little things that matter.'

John didn't believe it. How could leaving his spade out in the rain turn into a big thing that mattered? It just simply couldn't! Daddy must be wrong.

But now, just see what happened to one little thing!

It Was Only a Little Thing

John had a wooden cart that he had made himself. It was really rather good. He had bought a big wooden box from the grocer for sixpence, and he had begged the gardener for four old wheels. He had fixed the wheels on to bars of wood that he had nailed beneath the box, and he had put on a very good handle to drag the box along.

'Now it's a fine cart,' said John in delight. 'Look, Daddy!'

'Very nice,' said his Daddy. 'You will find it most useful.'

John did. He pulled Anna, his little sister all round the garden in his wooden cart, and he went shopping for Mother every day with it. He put the shopping into the cart instead of carrying it, and it was very easy to pull it along in that way. He could even bring potatoes and heavy goods like that, and Mummy was very pleased.

After John had used his wooden cart for about six weeks, one of the wheels began to wobble. Daddy noticed it at once.

'John, that wheel of yours will soon be off,' he said. 'It wants a new nail knocked in. Don't forget to do it.'

But that was just one of the little things that John couldn't be bothered to do. He'd do it tomorrow – or when the wheels came off – he just simply couldn't bother himself to fetch the hammer and nails and mend the wheel at once.

So of course he didn't do it. When

Mummy asked him to go and fetch her six pounds of carrots that morning, he looked at the wheel and thought: 'Well, I expect it will do one more journey. And, anyway, if it does come off there are still three for the cart to run on.'

Off he went, pulling his cart by the handle. He came to the greengrocer's and the man put the bag of carrots into the cart. Then away went John down the hill.

But he hadn't gone far before the wheel came off! It shot off and ran into the roadway. It rolled down the hill, jumping high in the air. A little dog, just about to cross the road, saw the wheel rushing at him and was scared. He gave a bark and rushed away from the rolling wheel, straight into the middle of the road, without looking up and down as he usually did.

A car was coming, and the little dog ran straight at it. The driver saw the dog, and hurriedly swung to one side, in case he should run over it.

Now the milkman was on the other side of the road, with his horse and cart and big milk churns. When his horse saw the car coming straight at it, it was frightened, kicked up its heels, and tore down the hill, with the milk churns rattling and the man shouting.

The horse couldn't stop when it came to the bridge at the bottom of the hill. It jumped over the low edge of the bridge

and fell straight into the canal below, dragging the milk-cart with it. The cart fell splash into the river, and the milk churns jumped off the cart, turned head-over-heels in the air, and neatly emptied themselves into the water.

The milkman fell into the water too. But he could swim, so he was soon out. Then the horse tried to swim out too, and at last a rope was fetched and the horse and milk-cart were dragged out: the cart was broken, and the milk was all gone.

'Whatever happened?' said a policeman in astonishment, taking out his notebook.

'My horse took fright because that car was driven straight at him,' said the milkman, pointing to a nearby car angrily.

'Well, I had to swerve aside because that dog almost ran into my car,' said the driver.

'And the dog got a fright because a runaway wheel rolled near him,' said a passer-by. 'It came off that little boy's cart.' He pointed to John, who was standing not far off, looking very white and scared.

'You should have the wheels of your cart on firmly,' said the policeman to John. 'Look what a lot of trouble your wheel has caused!'

John ran home, crying. All the carrots spilt as his cart bumped along on three wheels, but John didn't notice. He wanted to get home to his Mother.

His Daddy was there too, and he listened to John's tale with a grave face.

'It was one of the little things that sometimes turn suddenly into a big thing,' he said. 'If only you had nailed on that wheel when I told you to, none of this would have happened. Little things are as important as big things, John.'

'I know that now, Daddy,' said John, wiping his eyes. 'What can I do to make up for it all? Could I empty my money-box and give it to the milkman, do you think? Would that be a help?'

'I think it would,' said Daddy. 'The only thing to do when we have caused trouble is to try to put some of it right again. It's a good thing no one was hurt.'

So John emptied his money-box and took his money to the milkman. He told him all about the loose wheel, and said how sorry he was.

'I'm going to be faithful in the little things now as well as in the big things,' he said. 'I didn't believe Daddy before when he said that little things sometimes turned into big ones - but when I saw that little loose wheel turning into a big accident, I knew what he meant!'

So now John remembers the little things. Do you?

12

The Blown-Away Rabbit

There was once a small rabbit who was a very friendly creature. His name was Bobbin, and if you could have seen his white tail bobbing up and down as he ran, you would have thought his name was a very good one!

He lived just outside the farmyard, near the pond where the big white ducks lived. He used to play with the yellow ducklings, and they were very fond of him.

One day Waggle-Tail, the smallest duck, had a terrible fright. He ran away from the others, because he wanted to see if there was a puddle he could swim on all by himself. The pond seemed so crowded when all the white ducks and the yellow ducklings were on it.

Well, Waggle-Tail waddled off to where he saw the rain-puddle shining. It was a very nice puddle indeed. Waggle-Tail sat on it and did a little swim all round it, quacking in his small duckling voice.

The farm cat heard him, and left his seat on the wall at once. Young fat ducklings made wonderful dinners for cats - but usually the ducklings kept with the big ducks, and the farm cat was afraid then.

'A duckling on a puddle by itself!' said the big grey cat to himself in joy. He crept round by the wall. He crept round the pig-sty. He crouched low and waggled his body ready to jump - and just then the duckling saw him. With a

terrified quack he scrambled off the puddle and ran to find his mother.

But he went the wrong way, poor little thing. He went under the field-gate instead of under the gate that led to the pond. The cat crept after him, his tail swinging from side to side.

'Quack! Quack! Quack!' cried the yellow duckling. 'Quack! Quack! Quack!'

But his Mother didn't hear him. Nobody heard him - but wait! Yes -

somebody *has* heard him! It is Bobbin the little rabbit!

Bobbin heard the duckling's quacking, and popped his long ears out of his burrow. He saw Waggle-Tail waddling along – and he saw the farm cat after him.

'Waggle-Tail, Waggle-Tail, get into my burrow, quickly!' cried Bobbin. Waggle-Tail heard him and waddled to the burrow. The cat would have caught him before he got there, if Bobbin hadn't leapt out and jumped right over the cat, giving him such a fright that he stopped for just a moment.

And in that moment the little duckling was able to run into the rabbit's hole! Down the dark burrow he waddled, quacking loudly, giving all the rabbits there *such* a surprise!

Bobbin leapt into the hole too, and the friends sat side by side, wondering if the cat was still outside.

'I daren't go out, I daren't go out,' quacked poor Waggle-Tail.

'I will go and fetch your big white

mother-duck,' said Bobbin. 'I can go out to the pond by the hole that leads there. Stay here for a little while.'

Bobbin ran down another hole and up a burrow that led to the bank of the pond. He popped out his furry head and called to Waggle-Tail's Mother.

'The cat nearly caught Waggle-Tail. He is down my burrow. Please will you come and fetch him.'

So the big white duck waddled from the pond and went to fetch her duckling from Bobbin's burrow. She was

very grateful indeed to Bobbin for saving her little Waggle-Tail.

'Maybe some day I shall be able to do you a good turn too,' she said. And off she went, quacking loudly and fiercely at the farm-cat, who was now lying in the sun on the wall.

Now not long after that, Bobbin wanted to go and see Waggle-Tail - but when he put his nose out of the burrow he found that it was raining very hard indeed.

'You must not go out in that rain,' said his mother. 'Your nice fur will be soaked. Wait till it stops.'

But it didn't stop. The rain went on and on and on. Bobbin was very cross. 'I will borrow an umbrella,' he thought. So he went to his Great-Aunt Jemima, and was just going to ask her for an umbrella when he saw that she was fast asleep, with her paws folded in her shawl. But there was the big red-and-green umbrella standing in the corner!

Bobbin knew that no one should borrow things without asking, but he simply couldn't wait until Aunt Jemima woke up. So the little rabbit tiptoed to the corner and took the big old umbrella.

He scuttled up the burrow with it, dragging it behind him. He pulled it

out of the hole and put it up. My goodness, it *was* a big one!

Bobbin held on to the big crook-handle and set off down the hillside. It was a very windy day, and the big purple clouds slid swiftly across the sky. A great gust of wind came, took hold of the umbrella - and blew it up into the sky!

And Bobbin went with it! He was such a little rabbit that the wind swept him right off his feet with the umbrella - and there he was, flying along in the sky, holding on to the umbrella!

He was dreadfully frightened. He clung to the handle with his two paws, hoping that he wouldn't fall, but feeling quite sure that he would, very soon. Poor Bobbin!

The wind swept him right over the pond. The ducklings looked up in surprise when they saw the enormous umbrella - but how they stared when they saw poor Bobbin hanging on to it too!

'It's a rabbit, it's a rabbit!' they cried.

And Waggle-Tail knew which rabbit it was. 'It's Bobbin, my dear friend Bobbin!' quacked Waggle-Tail. 'Mother, Mother, look at Bobbin! He will fall. What can we do to save Bobbin? He saved me – we must save him!'

'But how can we?' said the mother-duck.

'Mother, can't you fly after him?' cried Waggle-Tail. 'I know you don't often fly, because you prefer to swim – but couldn't you just *try* to fly after poor Bobbin?'

'I will try,' said the big mother-duck. So she spread her big white wings and rose into the air. She flapped her wings and flew after the big umbrella. Bobbin was still holding on, but his paws were getting so tired that he knew he would have to fall very soon.

The mother-duck flew faster and faster on her great wings. She caught up the umbrella. She flew under the surprised rabbit and quacked to him.

'Sit on my back! Sit on my back!'

Bobbin saw her just below him. He

let go the umbrella handle and fell neatly on to the duck's broad, soft back – plop! He held on to her feathers.

Down to the pond she went, carrying the frightened rabbit. What a welcome the little ducklings gave him! As for Waggle-Tail, he could hardly stop quacking!

'You did me a good turn, and now my mother has paid it back!' he quacked 'Oh, I'm so glad you're safe!'

'So am I,' said Bobbin. 'But, oh dear,

what about my Aunt Jemima's umbrella? It's gone to the clouds!' It came down again the next day, and fell into the field where Neddy the donkey lived. Neddy took the handle into his mouth and trotted to Bobbin's burrow with it.

'Here you are!' he said to Bobbin. 'I heard that your Aunt Jemima was going to smack you for taking her umbrella without asking. I hope she hadn't smacked you yet.'

'No, she hasn't,' said Bobbin joyfully. 'Oh, thank you, Neddy! What good friends I have!'

He ran down the burrow with the big umbrella, meaning to give it to his Great-aunt Jemima. But she was asleep again, with her paws folded in her shawl: so Bobbin quietly stood the umbrella in the corner and ran off to tell Waggle-Tail.

'Don't get blown away again, will you, Bobbin?' begged the duckling. And Bobbin promised that he wouldn't. He didn't want any more adventures just then!

13

The Ladder That Was Lent

Mr. George was very generous with all his belongings. He was always lending people things, but he didn't always get them back.

He lent his spade to Mr. Jones, and his barrow to Mr. White. He lent his best basket to old Miss Lucy, and his biggest pail to Mrs. Jenks.

And then along came Mr. Hopps, one cold winter's day, and asked if he could borrow Mr. George's ladder.

'I've got a dead branch on my elm tree,' said Mr. Hopps. 'I'm afraid it will fall down on someone, Mr. George, so I want to climb up and saw it off before it does. I haven't a ladder, and I'd think it very kind of you if you'd lend me yours.'

'Well, certainly I will, Hopps,' said Mr. George generously. 'But do bring it back soon, there's a good fellow. You know, I haven't got my barrow back yet; and I can't do any digging, because Mr. Jones still has my spade. And I haven't even got a basket to collect my eggs in, because Miss Lucy has forgotten to bring it back.'

'Oh, I'll bring back your ladder at once,' said Mr. Hopps - and he quite meant to. He put the ladder over his shoulder and went off home with it. The next Saturday he put it up against his elm tree and sawed off the dead branch. It would make fine logs!

'I think I'll saw up this great branch now,' said Mr. Hopps, and he set to work. 'It would be a nice idea to give Mr. George a few logs too, in return for lending me his ladder!'

Well, that was a kind thought of Mr. Hopps, but I'm afraid it was only a thought. When he had finished sawing

up the branch, Mr. Hopps was very tired. He looked at the ladder and he looked at the logs, and he shook his head.

'I just can't take that ladder back to Mr. George to-day,' he thought. 'I'll take the logs *and* the ladder to-morrow. I must really go in and have a rest and a nice hot cup of tea now.'

So indoors he went – and forgot all about the ladder. A whole week went by and Mr. Hopps didn't think a single word about that ladder.

It was very cold weather. The snow came down and lay on the ground. The puddles froze up. The big village pond was frozen all over, and the children longed to slide on it.

Mr. Hopps's little boy wanted to go sliding too. But Mr. Hopps shook his head.

'No, Johnny,' he said. 'The ice isn't thick enough yet. You will fall in if you go sliding, because the ice will break.'

'I can't imagine why children want to go sliding on the nasty, cold, windy pond on a horrid day like this,' said Mrs. Hopps, shivering. 'I wish we had some logs to put on the fire. This coal burns badly.'

'I'll get you some logs,' said Mr. Hopps at once, remembering the logs he had sawn up the Saturday before. 'I've got some fine ones for you.'

He ran out into the garden and looked for the logs – and then he suddenly saw Mr. George's ladder

leaning up against the elm tree.

'Good gracious, there's Mr. George's ladder!' said Mr. Hopps in dismay. 'I said I would take it back at once, and I didn't. I forgot all about it.'

He took some logs in to his wife. She was pleased.

'Come in and sit down,' she said to Mr. Hopps. 'We will have a nice warm now.'

Mr. Hopps shook his head. 'I'm going to take that ladder back to Mr. George,' he said. 'I forgot all about it last week.'

'Oh, don't bother about that now,' said Mrs. Hopps. 'A day or two more can't matter. It's too cold to go out to-day. Besides, you're tired.'

'That's quite true,' said Mr. Hopps, looking longingly at the lovely fire. 'I *am* tired, and it *is* cold to-day. But I *must* take back that ladder, so good-bye.'

'Well, I think you are foolish to bother with that to-day,' said Mrs. Hopps, quite offended. Mr. Hopps went to get the ladder. He put it over his shoulder and set off.

On the way he had to pass by the village pond and he stopped to see if it was thickly frozen. A few children were on the ice, trying to see if it would bear them. One little boy was almost out on the middle of the pond.

'The naughty boy,' said Mr. Hopps – and then he saw that it was his son Johnny! And just as he was about to call him back, the ice broke with a loud crack, and poor Johnny disappeared into the bitterly cold water. He yelled for help, and tried to climb out – but he couldn't.

What a shock for Mr. Hopps! Whatever was he to do?

'A ladder! Fetch a ladder!' yelled somebody. And then Mr. Hopps remembered what he was carrying – a ladder, of course! So down on to the ice he laid it, quite flat, and pushed it gradually nearer and nearer to poor, cold Johnny.

Johnny reached out and took hold of the last rung of the ladder. Then Mr. Hopps pulled the ladder slowly back over the ice – and Johnny came too, pulled safely by the ladder.

'You naughty little boy!' cried Mr. Hopps, half angry and half upset. 'Go home at once to your mother and get dry!'

Off went Johnny, crying bitterly, for he was very wet and cold. Mr. Hopps hurried to Mr. George's with the ladder.

'How good of you to bring it back on such a horrid, cold day!' said Mr. George, pleased.

'Well, my wife didn't want me to,' said Mr. Hopps, 'but I really felt I must, Mr. George - and if I hadn't, why, I do believe my little Johnny might have been drowned. I was just going by the pond when he fell in - and as I had your ladder I was able to get him out with it.'

'That was a good reward for you for bringing my ladder back to-day, then,' said Mr. George, smiling. 'I wish everyone would return my things like you.'

'I'm going to send you some of my logs,' said Mr. Hopps. 'I won't forget.'

He didn't forget - and now Mr. George has fine wood-fires. As for Mr. Hopps, he never forgot that through taking back something he had borrowed, he was able to help his own little boy: and now when he borrows something, he gives it back at once. But all people aren't like that, are they?

14

Mr. Chunky's Chopper

Pincher Pixie was a bad little fellow. He was always taking things that didn't belong to him. This was a great pity, because Pincher Pixie had plenty of money and some very nice things of his own.

'It's just a bad habit of yours, taking things like this,' scolded Dame Flap, when she caught him taking a pot of jam out of her cupboard. 'You have a whole cupboardful of jam at home - much better jam than this is - and yet you must take a pot of mine! For shame, Pincher! You'll get into bad trouble one of these days.'

Pincher took Mother Goody's broom when he found that she had left it outside her kitchen door. He didn't

need it, for he had a good broom of his own – but he just simply couldn't help taking other people's things. No wonder nobody trusted him.

Now one day Pincher Pixie wanted some wood for his fire. He had a great deal of wood out in his yard, but it needed chopping up. Pincher Pixie went out to look at it.

'I guess that will make my arm tired,' he said to himself. 'What a nuisance chopping wood is!'

Just then he heard the sound of somebody else chopping wood. Pincher put down his own chopper and went to the bottom of his garden, where the noise came from. And there he saw a most peculiar sight!

Mr. Chunky was there - but he wasn't chopping wood. Oh no! And yet his wood *was* being chopped!

It was being chopped by a very peculiar chopper. This chopper was bright blue, and very large. It was working all by itself, lifting up in the air and chopping down on the wood without anybody helping it! Pincher stared as if he couldn't believe his eyes.

'Stop, Chopper,' commanded Mr. Chunky, when the chopper had finished the pile of wood. The chopper dropped to the ground with a clang. Mr. Chunky brought another pile of wood to it.

'Chopper, chopper, start to chop,
Chopper, chopper, do not stop,
Chopper, chopper, chop away,
Work for me by night and day!'

As he chanted these words to the

chopper, it lifted itself up, did a little dance of joy on its blue handle, and jumped to the pile of wood. It began to chop.

'Chop, chop, chop, chop, chop!' How that chopper chopped! It didn't stop for a minute. Pincher Pixie, who was peeping through the fence, was simply too astonished for words. If only he had that chopper, what a help it would be!

No sooner had the thought come to him than Pincher Pixie made up his mind to have the magic chopper. But how was he to get it?

An idea soon came into his head. He ran indoors to his telephone, and rang up Mr. Chunky's number. That would make Mr. Chunky's bell ring, and he would have to go to the telephone. He would have to leave his chopper - and Pincher would take it!

He asked for Mr. Chunky's number, then he left his telephone and ran down to the bottom of his garden again. As he went, he heard Mr.

Chunky's telephone bell ringing. He heard Mr. Chunky say, 'Bother! There's the phone! Stop, Chopper!'

Up his garden went Mr. Chunky, and as soon as he was out of sight, Pincher climbed over the fence, and ran to the chopper.

The pixie picked it up, went back to his own garden, and took the chopper to his wood-yard.

He put the chopper on a pile of wood and sang to it.

'Chopper, chopper, start to chop,
Chopper, chopper, do not stop,
Chopper, chopper, chop away,
Work for me by night and day!'

The chopper did a little dance very comically on the ground before it began to chop. Then it set to work. Pincher watched it in delight.

How it chopped! So quickly, so neatly, so well. It was marvellous! It chopped up the whole pile of wood, and then it chopped up the next pile. That was all the wood that Pincher had. As fast as the chopper chopped, the pixie piled the wood up neatly into the corner of his wood-shed. Soon there was a tremendous lot.

'Well done, Chopper,' said Pincher, as the chopper chopped the last piece of wood. 'Thank you. Now stop please, Chopper.'

The chopper stopped - but it didn't fall down to the ground with a clang this time. It seemed to look at Pincher, and it wasn't a very nice look. It danced a few steps towards a big garden broom that stood nearby.

And before Pincher could stop the chopper, it had chopped that broom into firewood! Yes - there was the

lovely broom lying on the ground in twenty small pieces!

'You stupid, silly chopper!' yelled Pincher in a rage. 'What did you do that for? Didn't you hear me say 'STOP'?'

The chopper stood still and looked at Pincher again. It seemed to the pixie as if it grinned wickedly at him. 'I said 'STOP'!' said Pincher again, feeling a bit afraid of the chopper.

The chopper danced about a little, and then hopped out of the wood-yard. It went to the garden-seat, and before Pincher could say a single word it had begun to chop it all up into small pieces! 'Chop, chop, chop, chop!' It chopped the back of the seat, and the legs - oh, there was no seat left by the time that chopper had finished!

Pincher was so angry that he ran at the chopper and tried to catch hold of it. But it suddenly turned on him and came hopping at him. Pincher felt sure it was going to chop at his shoes, so he ran away.

After that the chopper did just as it liked. It chopped up two deck-chairs. It chopped down all the trees in the garden and made them into logs. It chopped down the wood-shed, and then it began to chop down the fence!

Pincher was so miserable. Nothing would stop that awful chopper.

When it had finished chopping every thing in the garden, the chopper hopped to the kitchen door and went inside - and will you believe it, it began to chop up the kitchen table and the chairs!

Pincher began to cry. He rushed down to the bottom of the garden, and there he found Mr. Chunky staring in surprise at the fence, which had been chopped down.

'Chunky! Oh, Mr. Chunky! come and stop your chopper!' he wept. 'It's chopping up my furniture. Oh, come quickly.'

'Did you take my chopper then?' asked Mr. Chunky sternly.

'No,' said Pincher, telling an untruth. 'It just hopped into my garden by itself and began chopping.'

Mr. Chunky looked angrily at Pincher. He knew he was not telling the truth.

'Oh!' he said. 'Did it really? Then it must want to stay with you, Pincher. I wouldn't dream of taking it away if it hopped into your garden by itself.'

'Chop, chop, chop, chop!' went the chopper in the house. Pincher turned pale. 'It's chopping up my bed,' he sobbed. 'I told you a story, Mr. Chunky. I took your chopper myself, but when I told it to stop chopping it wouldn't. Do, do come.'

'You are a very bad pixie,' said Mr. Chunky, sternly. He walked up the garden and into Pincher's house. The chopper was chopping up Pincher's wash-stand into small bits.

'It is not supposed to stop chopping for anyone but me,' said Mr. Chunky to Pincher. 'That is why it would not stop when *you* told it to.'

'Oh, don't stand talking, tell it to STOP!' wept poor Pincher, seeing his cupboard being chopped up.

'Chopper, stop,' said Mr. Chunky. The chopper stopped and looked at Mr. Chunky. Mr. Chunky held out his hand. The chopper flew neatly into it and Mr. Chunky turned to go.

'What am I to do about all my beautiful furniture and garden-seat and shed?' cried Pincher in despair.

'Well, it's made into beautiful fire-wood,' said Mr. Chunky. 'You can burn it! Serves you right, Pincher. Maybe you won't take other people's things after this.'

And off he went, leaving Pincher to stare in despair at all his chopped-up furniture.

'Why did I take his chopper?' groaned Pincher. 'I'll never, never do such a thing again!'

I don't expect he will. He's still burning firewood made of his furniture, wood-shed, and fence. Poor, silly Pincher!

15

Bessie's Butterfly

Bessie had a cold. She had been away from school for three days, but Mother said she could go back the next day. So Bessie was very pleased, because she loved school.

'It's nature-lesson tomorrow,' she said. 'Good! I love nature-lesson. Miss Brown has asked us to see what we can bring for the nature-table tomorrow, Mother. I wonder what I can bring. Can I go out and see if I can find something this afternoon?'

'Yes, if it's fine,' said Mother. 'Maybe you will be able to find a little yellow coltsfoot, or perhaps a snowdrop in the garden, or a very early crocus or primrose. Or maybe you can pick some black ivy-berries. They are ripe now, and the birds are eating them.'

'Oh yes, there are lots of things to find,' said Bessie. 'I shall have my name on the nature-chart if I bring something that no one else has found. Billy had his name written on the chart last week because he brought a ladybird! Fancy that, Mother. You wouldn't think anybody could find a ladybird so early in the year, would you?'

'No, I wouldn't,' said Mother.

The afternoon came at last – and, oh dear, what a pity, it was pouring with

rain! Bessie looked out of the window and then went to Mother.

'It's raining,' she said, 'but I can put on my sou'-wester and mackintosh, can't I?'

'No, Bessie, I'm afraid you can't', said Mother. 'You might make your cold come back if you get wet again. You must play indoors.'

'Oh, Mother! But I shan't find anything for the nature-table, then,' cried Bessie sadly. 'It's too bad. I did so want to.'

'Darling, I'm sorry,' said Mother. 'But I simply can't let you get wet. I don't want you to have to go to bed again. Now cheer up - go and play in the attic, if you like. It is warm up there, because the hot-water tank is there, and you will be as warm as toast.'

Bessie liked playing in the attic. It had two funny little windows, a big pile of old trunks, a huge shelf of old picture-books, and the tiny cot Bessie had had when she was a baby. It was

fun to get into that and curl up and pretend she was tiny again.

But, oh dear, what a pity she wouldn't be able to find anything to take to Miss Brown next day! Well, it couldn't be helped. Bessie wasn't going to sulk and grumble. She knew Mother hated that.

So up the stairs she went and into the attic. It looked very dusty. Bessie thought it would be fun to put on an apron and cap, and pretend to be Jane the maid, cleaning hard. So downstairs she went again, found an apron, and made herself a cap out of a handkerchief. She borrowed a duster and a broom from Jane, and went up to do some cleaning.

And do you know what she found in a corner of the attic ceiling? A butterfly! Would you think anyone would find a butterfly so early in the year? Bessie couldn't believe her eyes! She had just been going to brush the cobwebs from the ceiling when she had seen the butterfly!

She looked at it - it seemed to be

asleep. She touched it. It fluttered its wings softly. So it was alive!

Bessie took it gently into her hand and went down to Mother with it. 'Guess what I've got!' she said. And she opened her hand and showed Mother the butterfly.

'A peacock butterfly!' cried Mother in surprise. 'It must have been sleeping the cold days away, up in our attic, Bessie. They sometimes do do that. How surprised Miss Brown will be to see a butterfly – that is far better than a ladybird!'

'I shall put it gently into a box with some holes in,' said Bessie, pleased. 'And to-morrow I'll take it to school. I'm sure I shall have my name on the nature-chart now! Oh, I am so pleased! What a good thing it poured with rain and I couldn't go out! I wouldn't have found the butterfly then.'

'And what a good thing you were nice about not going out, and went so cheerfully to play in the attic!' said Mother. 'Well – you deserve your butterfly, Bessie!'

Bessie's name is on the nature-chart! You can't think how proud she is to see it there!

16

The Hungry Little Robin

Far away in the country, at the bottom of a big hill, there lived a little old lady all alone. Her name was Dame Twinkles, and it suited her, for when she smiled her eyes twinkled in her face.

She was a kind old woman, and although she was very poor, she always had a carrot to spare for the donkey in the field nearby, and a few crumbs for the birds.

One day, when it was winter, there came a spell of bitter, frosty weather. All the ponds and puddles froze up and even the little stream. The ground was so hard that it was like iron. The farmer took his donkey out of the field, and put him into a warm shed.

'Dear, dear!' said Dame Twinkles, looking out of her window. 'What bitter weather! How are the birds going to get worms out of the ground, or find any seeds, now everywhere is frozen hard? And where will they get water to drink?'

Outside there were some poor, cold little birds, wondering if Dame Twinkles was going to give them any crumbs. The thrushes and the blackbirds could not peck anything out of the hard ground. The robin could find no insects. The sparrows had eaten all the seeds and berries there were. Worst of all, there was no water to drink!

Dame Twinkles nodded at the little things. 'I'll bring you water in a minute,' she said. 'And I'll put out a few plant-pots for you to roost in, with straw inside to keep you warm. And you shall have a fine cake all to yourselves!'

So she put out a big dish of water, and arranged some plant-pots on their sides here and there, with straw inside. She knew that many birds would sleep in the pots that night, especially the little tits, who felt the cold so much.

Then she baked them a fine cake of different seeds and currants and flour, and put it on an old tree-stump for them to eat. She cooked two large

potatoes in their skins and split them open for the birds to peck at. She hung up a bone for the tits and the starlings. Weren't they delighted!

'Isn't she kind, isn't she kind?' sang the big blackbird.

'She's sweet, sweet, sweet!' sang the thrush.

'Shall I tell her, shall I tell her?' asked the robin in his creamy voice.

'Yes, do, yes do,' said all the birds. They knew that the robin was the tamest and friendliest of them all. So the little robin flew to the window and tapped on it with his beak. Dame Twinkles opened the window in surprise.

The robin hopped into the room, sat on the mantel-piece and sang with all

his might to thank Dame Twinkles. She listened and nodded.

'I understand you,' she said. 'I am glad to help you, hungry little robin! Come and peck at the window whenever you want anything.'

So after that, whenever he and the other birds were hungry, thirsty, or cold, they sent the robin to peck at the window, and very soon he was so tame that he would perch on Dame Twinkles' shoulder and take crumbs from her mouth. She loved him, for he was a pretty, gay little thing with a beautiful voice.

One night that winter it began to snow. How it snowed! The flakes were as big as swan-feathers, and they floated down all night long. The wind blew the snow against the little cottage at the foot of the hill and piled it up around it, so when Dame Twinkles awoke that morning she wondered why her cottage was so dark.

'Why, the snow is right up against my window!' she cried. 'I cannot see

out! It must have been snowing all night long! I am snowed up!'

She dressed, and went to her front door. But she could not open it because of the weight of the snow against it. She was a prisoner!

'Good gracious!' said Dame Twinkles, afraid. 'What am I to do? I can't get out! Perhaps somebody will think of me, and come and dig me out.'

But nobody came. Nobody thought of the little cottage tucked away at the foot of the hill. All that day and the next night Dame Twinkles waited and waited - but nobody came to help her.

'If the snow does not melt, I shall starve here,' said the old lady to herself. 'It seems colder than ever. It might last for weeks!'

Now outside, the birds were wondering what had happened to the cottage, for it was half buried. On the second day, when no Dame Twinkles had appeared to give them food and water, the robin said he would try to find a window and peck at it.

So he scrambled through the snow and managed to make himself a passage to the window. He pecked on it.

'Tap-tap-tap!' Dame Twinkles jumped - then she saw that it was her hungry little robin. She opened the window and let him in. She gave him a few crumbs and a drink of water. He hopped on to her shoulder.

And then an idea came to Dame Twinkles. Suppose she wrote a tiny note, tied a piece of cotton to it, and bound it round the robin's leg, maybe

someone would see it, and perhaps rescue her! So she quickly got a small piece of paper and wrote on it. She gently took the robin in her hand, and tied the little note round its leg.

'Tirry-lee, tirry-lee!' said the robin in surprise, but he did not struggle, for he was not afraid of Dame Twinkles.

'Listen little friend,' said Dame Twinkles. 'Go to the farmer who lives on the other side of this hill, and let him take this note from your leg. I have been kind to you, and now it is right that you should do something for me.'

The robin carolled a little song and flew to the window. He understood perfectly for he was very tame. He made his way through the snow, and flew up into the air. He sang to tell the other birds what he was going to do, and then he flew off to the farm.

The farmer's wife was a cheery, kindly soul, and was singing a little song in her kitchen when the robin tapped hard at her window-pane.

'Bless us all, it's a hungry little

robin!' she said to the farmer, who was having his dinner. 'I'll let it in, and give it a bite to eat. Shoo, puss! Go into the hall or you'll frighten the robin!'

The cat shot into the hall. The door was shut on her. The farmer's wife opened the window and in came the robin. It flew to the table and sang to the farmer as loudly as it could.

'Well, here's a queer thing,' said the farmer, staring at the robin in surprise. 'What's it singing at me for?'

'It's got something wrong with its leg,' said his wife. 'Look - what's the matter with it?'

The farmer stretched out his hand, expecting the robin to fly at once, but it didn't. It stood there, half afraid, and let the farmer feel its leg.

'Why, it's paper,' said the farmer. He untied the note from the robin's leg and read it. 'Look my dear it's come from old Dame Twinkles to say she's snowed up, poor old thing. I must go and dig her out at once! Fancy her sending a letter by a robin!'

The farmer put on his hat and coat, took a spade, and went off through the snow to old Dame Twinkles. His strong arms soon dug away the snow from her door and windows, and made a good path for her to the gate.

'Oh, thank you, thank you!' cried the old lady. 'My little robin must have taken you the note very quickly!'

'He's a brave little thing!' said the farmer, looking at the robin, who was standing on the handle of his spade, flicking his wings. 'You're lucky, Dame Twinkles, to have a friend like that!'

'Tirry-lee! *We* are lucky to have a friend like Dame Twinkles!' sang the robin. 'Are you all right now, Dame Twinkles?'

'Quite all right,' said the old lady, smiling. 'And tomorrow I will bake you all a fine new cake for yourselves for a treat!'

So she did - and last time I passed that way the birds were *so* busy eating it!

17

Mother Minky's Trick

Mother Minky was a very good cook. She made pies and cakes, tarts and buns, and they were really most delicious.

She had a very broad window-sill, and she always put her goodies there to cool. She kept a sharp eye for the birds, who would dearly have loved to peck a bit out of a pie. Her cat, Snoozer, always lay below the window, to help Mother Minky to guard her baking.

Now one morning Mother Minky made four meat-pies, two apple-pies, six cherry-buns, and two currant-cakes. They were all as perfect as could be. The old dame put them out on the window-sill, and called to Snoozer the cat.

'Snoozer! Wake up for a while! There are plenty of things for you to guard this morning! Don't you let those greedy starlings come and steal, will you?'

'Mee-ow,' answered Snoozer, stretching himself and winking his yellow eyes at his mistress.

He lay and watched carefully. The birds saw his yellow eyes glinting, and they kept away. But when Mother

Minky came to take in her baking, she gave a cry of surprise.

'Snoozer! There is a meat-pie missing - and a currant-cake! Now what has happened to them?'

Snoozer sat up in astonishment. He knew quite well that no bird had been down to the sill - and how could

anyone else have taken the things? He would have seen them!

'You've been asleep, Snoozer,' said

Mother Minky crossly. 'That is very bad of you. You will have no dinner!'

'Mee-ow-ow-ow,' said Snoozer sadly. He knew that he had not been asleep – but however could that pie and cake have gone?

Now the next morning Mother Minky put out three jam-tarts to cool, and two chocolate-cakes. She called to Snoozer.

'Snoozer! Sit up and watch, please. My cakes and tarts are cooling on the sill!'

Snoozer sat up straight. He cocked his sharp ears and opened his yellow eyes wide. He watched and watched, putting his claws in and out, ready to leap at any bird that flew down.

But no bird came – and yet when Mother Minky came to take in her goodies, there was only one tart and one cake on the sill. The others had gone!

She was very angry indeed. She spanked poor Snoozer and told him he was a very naughty cat, and she couldn't trust him any more. Snoozer

waved his long tail about and felt dreadful. He knew quite well that he hadn't seen anyone taking those cakes - so how could they have gone?

Now the next time that Mother Minky put out her cakes, she watched them herself. And she saw a very strange and peculiar thing!

Snoozer was down below, watching in the garden. The cakes - four ginger ones and one large nut-cake - were cooling on the sill. Mother Minky saw them quite clearly and then, all of a sudden, two ginger-cakes leapt into the air and the nut-cake followed! They flew off round the garden, through the gate, and then were out of sight.

'Well!' said Mother Minky, most astonished. Her knees suddenly felt very weak, and she sat down on a chair. 'Never have I seen cakes do that

before! Where have they gone? Why did they go?'

Quickly she then leaned out of the window. 'Snoozer,' she called, 'did you smell or hear anything just then?'

'No-ee-oh,' answered Snoozer.

Mother Minky sat down again and thought. The cakes had flown off the window-sill, gone round the garden – *and gone out of the gate!* Now why should cakes go out of a gate? They didn't need to! They could quite well have flown over the hedge. Cakes didn't *need* to go out of gates, as people did.

'I think I know the answer to this riddle,' said Mother Minky at last. 'Yes, I think I know! The cakes didn't fly off by themselves – they were carried by somebody who couldn't be seen! He crept quietly to the window – lifted up the cakes – and then ran round the garden and through the gate. He must have been wearing a magic cap or cloak to make him unseen – the horrid little thief! Now I wonder who it is! I just wonder.'

But Mother Minky didn't know. 'I

mean to find out, though,' she said. 'Now what shall I do?'

She thought and thought. Then she rubbed her hands and smiled. Yes - she would use her blue-nose spell. She had had it for a long time and had never used it. Now it would be just the very thing!

So the next morning, when she made two big jam-tarts, she mixed the powdery blue-nose spell in with her flour. It was a curious blue colour, but it didn't show when the jam-tarts were baked. Mother Minky put the tarts on the sill as usual.

In half-an-hour's time those two tarts seemed to jump off the sill, fly round the garden, and go out of the gate. Mother Minky smiled. 'All right!' she said. 'You've gone, jam-tarts - but I'll soon know who's taken you!'

That afternoon Mother Minky sent out a message to say that she was giving a party, and please would everyone come to it. She would have it in the garden, and give everybody a good time. She set to work to make dozens of cakes and buns.

Everybody was pleased. They loved Mother Minky's parties because her cakes were so delicious. They put on party-dresses and went to Mother Minky's at four o'clock. Mother Minky looked quickly round her guests – yes, everybody was there!

'The blue-nose spell will begin to work soon,' she said to herself. 'Ha ha! The thief didn't know that there was a spell in those tarts that would turn his nose bright blue in six hours' time!'

The guests drank their tea and ate their buns. And then somebody pointed to a small brownie and began to laugh.

'Look! Look! Smarty has got a bright blue nose. Smarty, what have you done to your nose?'

Smarty was astonished. He was a mean little pixie with an ugly face. He looked at his nose in a glass. Good gracious! It was as blue as the sky! What could have happened?

'I don't like it,' said Smarty, fright-

ened. 'I think I'll go home. I don't know why my nose has gone blue.'

'But *I* do!' said Mother Minky in a sharp angry voice. 'Come here, Smarty, and I will tell you.'

The brownie came near. Everyone crowded round and listened. '*Some*body has been stealing my cakes, pies, and tarts each day,' began Mother Minky.

Smarty went pale. 'It wasn't me - it wasn't, it wasn't!' he cried.

'Be quiet,' said Mother Minky. 'Well, this morning I thought I would catch the thief - so I put a blue-nose spell into my tarts. Whoever ate those tarts would have a blue nose six hours later. And *you,* Smarty, have a bright blue nose!'

Well, Smarty was very frightened when he saw how angry everyone was looking. He knew he was in for a very good spanking! Quick as lightning he put on a little red cap - it was magic, and made him vanish at once!

'Now you can't see me, and I can escape!' shouted the bad little brownie.

But he had forgotten his blue nose! It was strong blue magic, and although all the rest of him had vanished, his blue nose still shone like a little blue stone in the air. So everyone knew where he was!

Smack! Spank! Slap! Smack! That naughty brownie was well spanked before he managed to get to the gate and run out. 'I shan't be able to sit down for a week,' he wept.

'And a good thing, too!' called Mother Minky. 'You'll keep that blue nose just

as long as you steal things, Smarty - so hurry up, and turn over a new leaf!'

Smarty didn't stay in that village a day longer. He was so ashamed. he packed up his things, put on his magic cap and, without being seen, ran off over the hills. But his blue nose could still be seen, and unless he has become honest, it is still wandering about the world like a little blue stone, about as high as your shoulder.

So if you see it, catch hold of it - and you'll have a brownie by the nose!

18

Micky's Present

One day Miss Brown, the children's school teacher, spoke to the children rather sadly.

'You will be sorry to hear that poor little Ronnie is very ill,' she said. 'He will have to lie in bed at least two months, and he will not be allowed to see anyone for a long time.'

The children were sorry. 'Can we do anything to make things nicer for him?' asked Jane, who was always the first to be kind.

'Well,' said Miss Brown, 'you might buy him a book or two when you have the money – or jigsaw puzzles perhaps. Something like that, it will be very dull for the poor little boy.'

Micky listened to what Miss Brown said. He was very fond of Ronnie, because he and Ronnie loved the same things. They never wanted to go into the hot, stuffy cinema on Saturdays as so many of the others did - they loved to go out together into the country lanes and fields and watch the birds and animals there.

Once they had seen a grey squirrel hiding his nuts. Another time they had found a prickly hedgehog, and he had rolled himself up into a ball as soon as he had seen them coming. They often listened to the birds singing, and Micky told Ronnie what they all were. They watched the rabbits playing in the evening, and had a much better time than the children who had gone to the cinema.

Micky felt very sorry for Ronnie. Now he wouldn't be able to watch the birds and animals as he loved to do. 'I shall miss him dreadfully,' thought Micky. 'I will take him a present.'

But Micky had no money to buy a

present. He didn't even get ten pence a week, because his mother was very poor. Micky asked her if he could have some money to get Ronnie a book or a puzzle.

'I haven't the money to spare,' said his mother. 'You know I had to buy you a pair of new boots last week, Micky.'

'Well, Mother, couldn't you even spare me some money for a "Sunny Stories"?' asked Micky. 'I could just get that for Ronnie. He does so like the stories in it you know.'

'Not twenty, not ten, not even one penny,' said his mother, firmly. 'If you want to give Ronnie something, you must give him one of your own toys.'

Micky went to look at his toys - but, dear me, they were a very poor, broken lot! 'They're not fit to give to anybody,' thought poor Micky. He sat and wondered about Ronnie. It must be horrid to lie in bed day after day, with only the clouds to watch moving in the sky. How he would miss the birds he loved!

And then, as Micky sat and thought, such a splendid idea came to him. He leapt up and clapped his hands.

'Of course! I'll make him a bird-table and fix it up just outside his bedroom window if his mother will let me! I'll put food on it every day for the birds, and Ronnie can lie and watch them and be happy.'

Making a bird-table didn't cost Micky

even one penny. He took a piece of wood from the shed, and looked about for a stick for a leg. His mother gave him an old broom handle. Just the thing! He nailed the flat piece of wood on to the leg. There was the table!

He put it over his shoulder and marched off to Ronnie's house. Ronnie's bedroom was downstairs. Micky saw

Mrs. Leslie in the garden, and he spoke to her.

'Please, Mrs. Leslie,' he said, 'I've got a present for your Ronnie. It's a bird-table. May I put it up just outside his window? He does so love the birds, you know.'

'How very kind of you, Micky!' said Mrs. Leslie. 'Poor old Ronnie feels so dull now, lying in bed day after day. He is tired of his books and puzzles. He will love to watch the birds.'

Micky put up the table just outside Ronnie's window. Ronnie was fast asleep, so Micky tried not to make any noise. He dug a hole for the broom-handle, and then fixed it hard in the earth, treading it down firmly. The top of the table was just above Ronnie's window-sill. He would be able to see the birds beautifully when they came.

'Mrs. Leslie, I'll go out into the lanes each Saturday and find some things that the birds love to eat,' said Micky. 'They'll love berries, you know, and seeds of all kinds. I'll collect lots! And

I'll ask my uncle for one of his big sunflower heads – that can go on the table too. The birds will come to peck out the seeds. And if I can get a few monkey-nuts, I will. The tits love those.'

'You're a kind fellow, Micky,' said Mrs. Leslie. 'Ronnie will be so pleased.'

Micky ran home, wondering what

Ronnie would say when he woke up. And what *did* Ronnie say? He was simply delighted! His mother had spread some crumbs on the table, and already one robin and three sparrows were hopping there.

'Mother! Who gave me that?' cried Ronnie in delight. 'Oh, what fine fun I shall have every day watching my birds! I shall soon know every one.'

Each day the table was spread with bits and pieces - bones for the starlings, bread for the robins, scraps for the sparrows, bits of potato for the thrushes and blackbirds. They all came and pecked hungrily. Then Micky brought berries and seeds - and you should have seen how the birds loved those!

When the doctor came in two weeks' time he was surprised to see how much better Ronnie was looking.

'He seems so bright and happy,' he said to Mrs. Leslie. 'That is splendid.'

'Look - this is what keeps him so interested and happy,' said Mrs. Leslie, and she showed the doctor the bird-

Micky's Present

table. On it were seven starlings, four sparrows, one robin, two chaffinches, three tits, one blackbird, and one thrush - and really, the table could hardly hold any more!

'What a good idea!' said the doctor. 'No wonder Ronnie looks so bright. I really think, Mrs. Leslie, that he might have a friend to tea next week, just to cheer him up a bit.'

Ronnie was so pleased - and whom do you suppose he asked to come to tea? Yes - Mickey, of course - and together the two friends watched the birds having their tea at the same time.

'It was kind of you to give me such a lovely present as that, Micky,' said Ronnie.

'Well, it wasn't much of a present,' said Micky. 'It didn't cost even a penny.'

'It's the nicest present of the lot!' said Ronnie. 'You took the trouble to think of what I really would love, Micky - and I do love it too. It's my favourite present.'

It was rather a good present, wasn't it? It would be lovely if every girl and boy could have a bird-table to watch – they really are such fun!